CALVIN DREAMS

"And that he will be bigger than the moon!"

JOY HOULDER

For my little brothers,
follow your dreams

CALVIN DREAMS

When Calvin is ready
for bed,

Mommy and Daddy
ask what Calvin will
dream of.

Maybe,
Calvin will dream
of planets
and stars.

And that he will
be bigger
than the moon!

Or maybe,
Calvin will dream
he is not so big.

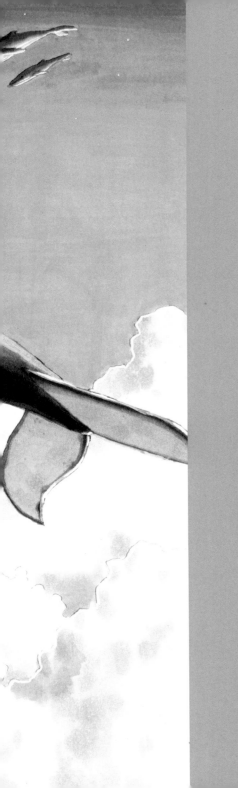

And that he is
flying with
huge whales!

What else
can this sweet child
dream of?

Yummy Treats!

After a treat,
calvin must dream
of adventure.

Does Calvin dream
of bravely finding
a bright world
in a dark forest?

Or perhaps,
Calvin dreams
he is shy.

Calvin spies
on the dancing aliens
in his backyard.

Don't be shy,
Calvin.
Say hello!

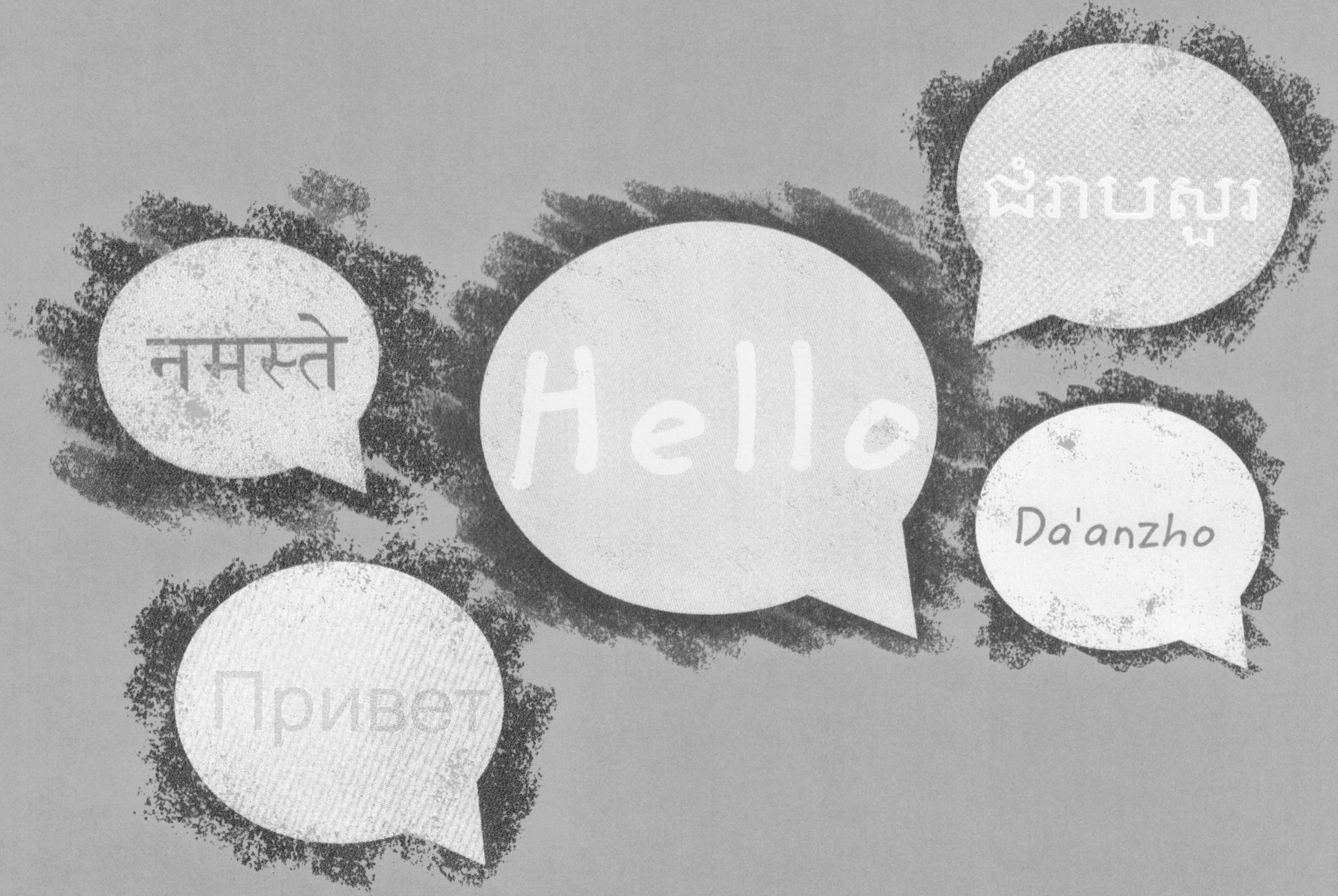
नमस्ते
Hello
ជំរាបសួរ
Da'anzho
Привет

The flowers say hello!

And before Calvin wakes,
does he dream of family
in the sky?

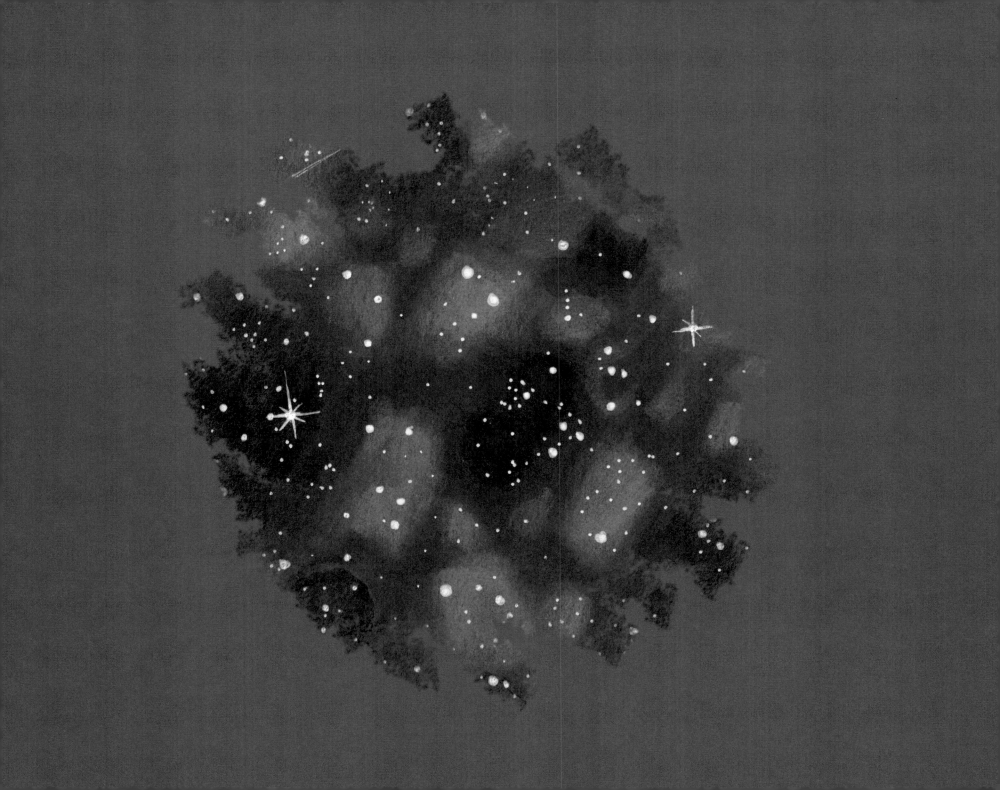

Grandma loves
when Calvin dreams
of visiting her.

In all,
Calvin will have
wonderful dreams
tonight.

Sweet dreams,
Calvin.

ABOUT THE AUTHOR & ILLUSTRATOR

Joy Houlder is the author and illustrator of *Calvin Dreams*.

Joy began creating *Calvin Dreams* shortly after the birth of her younger brother, Calvin Houlder. Joy realized that there were not enough playful and magical books for children of color so she envisioned Calvin having his very own book to see himself in. Calvin provided Joy the drive to create a children's book that uplifts children of color with the incorporation of dreams, fantasy, and possibility. Joy is currently working on more projects with whimsical and positive images of people of color in art and literature.

Calvin & Joy Houlder

CALVIN
DREAMS

Lightning Source UK Ltd.
Milton Keynes UK
UKRC020043121219
355180UK00002B/2